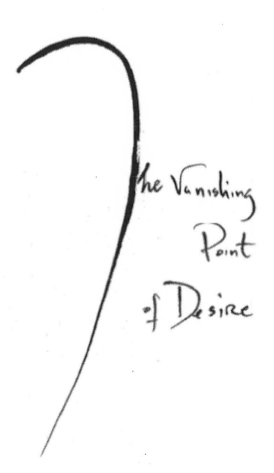

The Vanishing Point of Desire

Vi Khi Nao

PER SECOND PRESS
P.O. BOX 2704
Iowa City, IA 52244
www.persecondpress.com

Per Second Press books may be purchased for educational,
business, or sales promotional use.
Please email :
persecondpress@gmail.com

Cover design by Bradley Paynter

Third Edition

ISBN 978-0-692-43632-5
Library of Congress Control Number: 2015950723

PER SECOND PRESS

IOWA CITY, IA

THE VANISHING POINT of DESIRE

V
I

K
H
I

N
A
O

for you

who is
you?

you
in
poem?

self?

everyone
of us
same?

are we the conference room?

In the conference room, a door opens. And closes. Like white culottes opening the curtain of their skirt. I think of the airport Charles de Gaulle. The window. The door. The bright afternoon light. Where flight attendants in mini-skirts wheel their luggage to and fro. Where paintings are suspended from the ceiling. The Tree of Solitude. The House of Intimacy. The

Vanishing Point of Desire. Inside the conference room, you are wearing a blue blouse sitting perpendicular to me. Any closer and our shoulders collide.

I take you inside. The empty wall. The vacant seat. The nonexistent hallway. Let me lay you down on my pillow of desire. Sleep. The gloaming is out of sight. Let me take you inside me.

I look at you. Look at the center of your opal body. Your bright face. The room slits in half. The room throbs in vulnerability. I descend the stairs. The moment. The stairs of Air France. The aluminum steps glitter in the sun. The sun is bright. Wearing his yellow hat, a halo of civilization. I descend the stairs and imagine you a Pear. A Lime. A Blue Fruit.

We are no longer talking. We are no longer talking about universities. The sun is too bright. Too kind. I gaze into your eyes. You are thinking perhaps of civilization. The continent of Africa. I am thinking it's Sunday. You are the Cathedral. I should walk in. Be mystical and religious and burn votives.

I am still descending the stairs. My white dress is caught in the moment. My right foot half in midair. I am dreaming of washing the Blue Fruit in my kitchen sink. Washing it with a cold coat of water. The water spilling over your body. I am holding you in the palm of my hand. I am holding you as the water gently blesses you with the hem of its skirt. I wonder what it's like to be underneath the skirt. It's, I think, where time parts his fluid lips. Time falls from the faucet onto your blue body and lands his kisses on you. He touches you with reverence. The hem of the skirt makes circular sweeps around your body.

Time, the Gentleman, handles you with reverence.

I am holding you as time washes over you. I see the window and door from the corridor. The wide hallway. The confetti carpet divides my attention as my eyes gloss over the intimate details of the airport's airless environs. I feel strange. Empty handed. And realize it's the first time I have traveled without a single piece of luggage clinging to my side. The lightness takes a moment of adjustment. My arms, my back, my shoulders hushed in levity.

Your blue body cradled in the palm of my hand. I turn off the faucet. Time stops kissing you. He has been all over you. The continent of Africa. Denmark and the Netherlands. Places I want to go or travel one day. I turn him off so he can catch his breath.

In the conference room, I gaze at you. You are wearing your blue blouse. It's a light blue. I think I like it on you. Your blue blouse does not look very blue. You have an ethereal quality about you that makes me want to handle you like Time, the Gentleman.

I ask, Was it breakfast that you dined with her?

You think for a moment. Words usher hesitantly out of your lips. It was not breakfast. Or was it lunch? Actually it was dinner. I cleared out my class schedule to attend that dinner with her. A petite soft-spoken woman walks out of your lips.

I do not know what to do with her but stare at you. In vexation. In amazement. She is dressed from top to bottom in spoken language. What do I say to language when she exits your lips? I softly, but quietly, resort to reticence.

You smile brightly narrating the dinner. I wonder if you know what a fork is while taking her in. The sexiest literary Aphrodite in the world. The woman whom you dined with writes in her notebook. She *is* notebook. She *is* writer. She *is* language. She looks awfully postmodern. Gigantic publishing companies do not know what to do with her, but bash her. Left and right. And years later embrace her.

She takes them in innocently. Like a mother with a spoiled child.

I walk you over to the dinning table. A white cloth dabs gently on your blue body. How do I serve you, I think? I place the Blue Fruit on a plate. This is the only time you get to be a dish. The half-dried cloth lies like a canopy on the five tips of my fingers. I twirl it while deciding. The bright light burning my sight.

The window. The door. The corridor.

Flight attendants in knee-high skirts walk to and fro on the terminal floor. The wheels of their luggage vacantly rolling. They know every inch of the floor. Their eyes seeing every secret. Every speck. Every crack.

It's beautiful to watch them roll. The heels click on the ceramic floor. The power of that city made of arrivals and departures. It's a city that runs on farewell and hello. This is the city in which I must meet you.

Charles de Gaulle— Window. Door.

The palimpsest of desire opens her body like a corridor. Time, the Gentleman, walks in first. I stay outside the pages, studying the text written in black ink. I hope he doesn't age you with his sweet, succulent lips. Strands of words hang loosely.

Around—

The strands —of desire. The gentleman takes too long. I am walking to and fro. Anxious.

You cease talking about the university. The dinner. The writer with her notebook. I do not know what to say to you. I am in a bath of reverence. The large dark maroon handbound book stares back at me. My drawings and paintings are still in there. Waiting. You have only glanced at the preliminaries. I have derailed. The train of the conversation descends into the bosom of fog. I wonder where we are in the interview. The diaphanous window of the conference room glows with light. Drowning it in innocence. The afternoon sun throws in his yellow halo hat. It lands on the hooks of the curtain. On the table. On the floor. The room slits open.

You are so quiet and I am so quiet. 16 Must I enter you? You in your blue blouse. I am in my red sweater. *Flowers of*

Shanghai.

I wonder if you have seen the movie called *Red.* Called *Blue.* We are making a movie called *White.* You smile because you have not seen Flowers or Shanghai in the same sentence. You think this is beautiful. Because you are so quiet and I am so quiet. Hsiao-hsien. I innocently gaze at you. I do not think I am very innocent. Thinking, contemplating walking into the Cathedral.

Without votives. Just wearing a white dress. Perhaps not wearing anything at all. Drowning in blue. My red. Your blue. Four elegant brothels. A courtesan in her prime.

The opium pipe of ink runs through the river of your breath. You inhale. I exhale. A trail of reddish brown, the drug, unravels the air. I am still outside the corridor. Time, the Gentleman, still inspects the palimpsest of desire. He takes his time. He looks carefully at the torn pages. The slit. The mark of passion. The pipe of ink. The opium floats through his nose.

I sit with you in intoxication.

For three years I have not had the pleasure of this moment. For three years I have not had a minute of intoxication with you. In the conference room, I experience two minutes. Two folds. You are Charles de Gaulle. The window. The door. I walk into you.

Descending the aluminum stairs to show you my drawings. My paintings.

I open the kitchen cabinet looking for something to feast upon with the Blue Fruit. A jar of honey sits among the clear canisters of peppercorn, aniseeds, cardamom, capers, flour, rock sugar, mung beans. The assorted scents of spices float out of the cabinet.

The beauty of a kitchen.

The Blue Fruit on the table. The pale amber color of the honey jar. Something is missing, I think, as I sit down at the dining table.

You are still very quiet. This is a sacred time, holding you as I undress the interview in the kitchen. The Blue Fruit dancing in my eyes. I am watching Shanghai wake up on the television screen. Flowers are blooming out of the brothel

floors. Jasmine. Jade. Pearl. Emerald.

Women fading in and out of dark paneled walls. Foods leaving and entering Asian men's mouths.

In two minutes. The eternity of desire stretches forever into time. I begin to undress the passion of the moment. The room slits open. Bright light burns my eyes. The window. The door. Is it my imagination, or are you really opening? As I walk down the corridor. The terminal is not a terminal. The wall is not the wall. Squandering the love of a woman is not my cup of tea as I turn on the stove. I fancy eating the blue fruit with Jasmine. The flower that sprouts out the brothel chamber.

The gas burner ignites. The knob rotates. Heat burns, spreads red, spreads blue. The two slivered colors released out of the nozzle, dancing, singing with its red, blue tongue flickering.

I turn on the faucet. Water runs down in fast spurts. Time has ceased inspecting the palimpsest of desire. He is filling up the vessel of the

metal teapot the shape of a Pear. I wonder what he thinks of the ripped pages. The dark marks. The strands of loneliness on the effaced surface. Can he read the writing, make out the lonely words? He is time, the Gentleman. He should be able to read himself at another time in his time.

The teapot sits on the burner. The tongue flickers on its bottom. Red and blue fan out. The conference room is on my mind. Shanghai is very near. Come here, I tell you. My eyes eyeing you. You are at the very end of the terminal. I pass by customs; my passport is at home. Flowers peel themselves off and fall onto the floor like tears. Red tears falling. Falling and halting mid-air.

Come here. The room slits open like a slit on a skirt. To open the culottes. To view the window. The window. The door. The bright light. The conference room. The airport Charles de Gaulle. I do not rip open your skirt. It is the hands of time, that Gentleman. Mistaking the slit on the earth's floor for your skirt. You must pardon him.

I part the curtain. He has created an orifice for me to enter. I dive my entire body into the slit.

The opening. The red bleeding into the blue. The tongues singing at the bottom of the teapot.

The burn. The throb.

The slit is the size of a passionate, sizeable ink stroke. It's the new stain on the body. On the palimpsest of desire. On the derailed interview in the conference room. On this quiet afternoon. The other side of the wall, a handful of scorers read essays. Madly. Vacuously.

With delicious boredom.

Come here. My hands quietly extend out to you. I am at the end of the terminal and the entrance into the Gallery. Your long fingers fall into my mind. I desire to take you into the Tree of Solitude. Let me take you there. Your fingers locking with mine.

The Tree of Solitude is Rilke's Solitude.

Marriage lives inside this parameter. This space that houses intimacy. The marriage of mind. The marriage of body. The marriage of spirit. This is the space inside the Tree that you are walking in with me. You are safe here, I think.

The Tree of Solitude is an ink painting on a large Kochi paper. The trunk is a large pipe branching out other smaller pipes, curling and shooting into

the vast sky. Leaves of words hang on the branches. Some words begin to defoliate.

Some words do not have time to defoliate—perch on the tree branch like a woman on a bleak autumn afternoon. Her pale bosoms exposed to the cold.

She dangles off the branch. On the edge of falling, but does not fall.

Those that do fall—suspend mid-air. The artist. The painter lifts the skirt of Autumn— Halting her from fully descending. The pen tip imposes his will on the leaves. The pen tip determines the length of the leaves. The length of each Word that embodies the tree.

The white dress. The blue fruit on the plate. I wonder if you have ever gazed at Autumn and desired her.

Sit down on the floor of the earth, I suggest to you as we walk into the painting. Sit down and let the skirt folds onto the bodies of words. Let the Tree of Solitude be your awning, your shade, your lover. Allow me to peel off your

black high heels. I will protect you, I assure you.

Women with their bosoms exposed will not fall on you. Trust me, I say. I am the creator. I impose my will on the pen tip. You bend down cautiously, your skirt lacing the earth's floor. Your back pinning to the tree's trunk, his pipe sings out words of—

Desire Despair Sadness Want

Could you hear his heartbeat drumming on your spine? Could you see his sweet lips? The mellifluous leaves lingering on the edge, on the verge of falling.

But do not fall. Women do not fall off trees. Not like that.

I prostrate myself on the earth. The white dress fans out. My knee crushing, digging deep into Words. The sacred text of the tree. You look at me as I peel your high heels from your feet. Your legs are long and luscious. Your black panty hose clinging. Clinging. Clinging to the curves of your legs. My hand clings to you too as I lift your first leg and place it on my thigh.

I gently remove the first high heel. I will protect 23 you, I assure you, baptizing your foot. Consecrating it.

Realizing I did not bring a pitcher of water with me, I bend down. With my hands, I cup the leaves and pour the Words onto the whiteness of your foot. In this moment, I bless you. I place this foot down and begin to administer baptism on your other foot. You close your eyes to inhale the sensuality, the calmness, and the equanimity of the afternoon. Your eyelashes fan out. Your lips supple and young.

You open your eyes and gaze into mine.

I ask you, have you ever looked at Autumn and desired her?

Your piercing blue eyes dancing. Must you pierce me like that, I ask you? Must you? With one gaze, you slit my soul open. Will the Tree of Solitude protect us from rain, I wonder? Your eyes are thinking, while mine are dreaming.

We make quite a pair on the sea of desire. It had been raining the day I met you. The Delphic clouds. Opaque and pale.

Saturated the entire celestial canvas. Like a dampened gloaming. The rest of the afternoon undressed itself quite hypnotically.

I discovered you at the bottom of a hotel called Highlander. It housed temporarily the New York project training section. My first project working under you. You stood there in your 6-foot stature, wearing your knee-high skirt. The color of your blouse won't come to mind. You were teaching us how to match words with numbers. I sat in the very back while graphs and pie charts ascended the stairs of my mind. I did not recall if they ever descended. But in my memory's eyes, their footsteps marked the beginning of the discovery of you. To variables and diagrams, I toast this unforgettable encounter.

The basement of the hotel did not have any windows and doors. A place to crunch in numbers and suffocate. Sitting in the back near the entrance door to the stairs, I felt dizzy and lightheaded. Words, numbers, chairs hung above my head like apples on a tree. I watched their globular heads clouding my mind. Where they saw me but I did not see them.

I remembered the room being soaked red. Velvet red. Like being inside of the theatre. The red carpet. The red wall. The color of pellucid Autumn. Individuals with their lead pencils and highlighters colored their training packets. Their hands moved right and left and left and right imitating the mechanics of a typewriter. You stood up front, which from my view, was the back of the room teasing the projector for not behaving like a docile apparatus. Your seraphic smile caught everyone's attention. In that moment, I hardly noticed anyone but

I noticed you.

The projector light radiated upon your face in the dark room. The lighting of this room cracked the space in half, mirroring the amphitheatre in Pompeii. Bestowing light to one side. The other half breathing in the shadow. You were the opal at the end of the tunnel. You looked like something I would walk into.

Indeed you were teaching geometry to shadows.

I was at the back of the room behind many tables and chairs looking very distant. My eyes focused on the transparent pitcher sitting at my table. Little pockets of water glided down the cylinder object before becoming little pools on the table surface. I was sitting next to the woman whom I was dating at that time. Being a massage therapist, she informed me that everyone here exemplified terrible sitting postures. I imagined reading essays with a houseful of corrupted flesh. It did not limn a pretty picture.

It was too early in my scoring profession for me to repine. I was young and naïve. A neophyte to the labor force. I had just been plucked out of the tree of education. A half-polished, unwashed, inorganic guava on an assembly line with other guavas. Rolling, tumbling. A few years down the road, when I saw my reflection on the more polished, luminary guavas, I discovered a woman I hardly recognized.

A flesh devoid of passion and youth.

And then opalescent you standing in that crimson background. Your face incandescing with youth and beauty and bliss. I thought you were a fata morgana. That perhaps you were an impalpable material emerging out of the carpel of an ancient flower.

No, you were not immaterial. You. An opal. An orchid. An impala. Solid. Soft. Elegant.

Like now as I view you. Somatic you. From my desk while reading a stack of essays. To assure that you are as real and as possible as my mind could apprehend, I bring you an essay I have been struggling to focus upon. I walk away to

give you the space to read.

I met you on a Fall, pluvial day. The darkest day of the year. Entering you. Entering the mouth of a cave. Entering into the darkness of my feelings. I wonder if you remember that day. The day where life was the color of scarlet. You had bruised me with the kiss of your presence. Feel my discolored skin. The red pulsation inside the guava.

The distillation. The refraction. Pixilated body. Pixilated mind.

The face of outdoor looking, searching, piercing inside me. Find me its new haven.

The foggy cloud. The bleak atmosphere. The ethereal gloaming. Diffusing across the body of my thoughts.

Spread me open and you will see. Spread me apart and you will see. The red darkness inside. The opal dancing at my feet.

And I recognize again, this woman facing me. She is palpable. In your opal reflection, a passionate scream.

Breaking. Singing. Erupting.

Out of the cracked body of the guava.

The seed of passion. The seed of love. The seed of sadness.

I met you on a fall day. When I was young. A sapling. Did you taste me? On that bleak autumn day. Did you suck on that seed? That nubile flesh.

You should. You ought to. It fermented out of your red lips. It has been cultured out of your tall tree.

You standing tall handing me back the essay. Very gently. Very quietly. You tell me what you think of it. I disagree with you just slightly. A point in organization. A minor variance in what we think constitutes clarity. You meet me half way.

I find that I gravitate towards your diplomacy. You are a master negotiator.

Will you negotiate with the seed inside me? Gently tell it to be quiet. Just a little. For my sanity. For my purity. For my security.

Will you tell it to germinate slowly? But with agility.

Tell its pink pulp to not swell too much. I fear it might burst inside of me. But especially to tell it to be quiet. Very quiet.

You walk away after the negotiation. A quiet exchange occurs between us. But

it means everything to me. The clarity of your presence. You have held the paper in the palm of your hand. Words indeed escape your lips. We converse.

I say You say I say You are palpable. You are
authentic. You are provocative.

In a phone conversation once when I, on an impulse,
asked you what you thought constitutes good writing.
When I was lost and couldn't make it out of the forest
of words. When I was at the end of my rope. When I
had just awakened from a whipping by a man who
lives inside of my head. You said good writing is
authentic.

Is this what you mean? By authentic. The guava. Your
red lips. The sweet kiss. Streamlining the

desire of an essay. The body of passion. The syntax of a woman. An original of my own. You are no one else but my own. My creation.

You asked me if that made any sense. If I understood what you meant. With confidence, I said, yes. Now, facing the ghost of solitude, I question if I knew what you meant. I question if I had been too quick, too capricious in discerning the essence of that which is genuine and that which is pseudo. Since I am one to live in many regrets, I regret not extending the conversation longer. I wish I had asked you what the antipode of authenticity was. Sometimes describing the negation of a concept enhances the quality of its meanings.

I wish I had negated with you. Perhaps our conversation would have more volume. Perhaps I realize that I can enjoy losing my body of reality with you. That this guava can burst quietly. That you will hold me on the tip of your tongue. That while words are floating, absconding from your lips, I am cascading on the back of your undulating tongue.

That you can suck on me. Swallow me. Allow me to be inside of you. Hold the same breath with you.

And I think I am dreaming. The conversation has to be short. Because I am incapable of letting you taste me. Because you haven't opened windows or doors to let me in. Because I am dying passionately. Quietly. Drowning even.

And always with a great deal of despair.

Authenticity lives in the city of phantoms. She rises occasionally to flaunt her ghost. Her elegant, diaphanous gown. And when she is finished with teasing, enticing, seducing, she submerges her lovely head 1000 fathoms into the depth of the sea. This is her enigma. I won't fathom gripping her slippery body. Or write her out like a text. She moves in and out. One day she will dip inside like the tip of a pen.

She will squirm like a black squid— On my journal. On my Kochi paper.

I pray then that your lips are sealed. Threaded tight. Because your tongue will become a prisoner of my mouth. Because you will taste me.

You will taste the throbbing pink pulp of authenticity— Moving in and out on your tongue. 32

Till it's numbed. And bounded by my passion. My kiss. My ink stroke. The pulp singing, bursting, drowning in the small pool of your saliva.

Each word is a stroke on your tongue. Our tongues undulating on each other's back. Clashing like waves. Pulling and tugging like ribbons. Tied unfashionably like a bow.

And I will ask you, is this what you mean by authenticity? Is this what it's like to savor it on the body of language?

To burn. To dance. On the edge of desire. Will you swallow this guava?

Will you? Let its pink pulp enter you. Be inside you.

Perhaps it's your turn to experience regret.

I met you at the bottom of a hotel on an autumn day. You the opal. I the guava. We alone are authentic enough.

What we do, manifest, become of each other. That is writing. 33 This is what I do. I write. On the Tree. The Tree of Solitude. I walk through life soaked in this tank of ink. This vessel of darkness. It's because of your father's death that I am painting and drawing again. I gaze at you in the conference room. The room lights differently. I am the ink bottle and you are the ink. I am dipping my pen inside you and removing a part of me from you.

Let me draw *you* with my pen. A drawing of Words.

She dips her pen in ink and the ink becomes a part of the pen. A woman coated in charcoal appears on the bleak white pages. A man stands right next to her measuring the centimeters of her chin, her pubic hair with his white hands. And he feels like a ghost and she is his substance. The negative of the other side. A penis appears. And she takes the eraser. For the penis is covered too much in charcoal. She takes the eraser and begins to reduce his penis. The scrotum must go. So must the mushroom head. But she doesn't have time to reduce it—and the toy is left with one last touch, one last line that finishes the entire picture of the sperm-making machine. The line between art and the artist becomes indiscernible.

She dips the pen in ink again. The bottle wobbles upon her touch. She has reduced the pen to its ink. She has called the ink various names. Ink you not pink. Ink you must sink. Ink. Ink. Ink.

She dips the pen in ink to write on the body of the woman. She writes on the body:

She places her lover on the swing. She swings her. She spreads her legs apart and with her heels in the air— and the tidal movement of desire—it comes and goes, moves in, moves out of the current of her mouth. Her tongue like the wave taps into the center of the "oyster shell" of the vaginal wall. She dips her tongue in. She is swung back. Each dipping brings her closer to the pulsation of desire.

Her cunt throbs in her mouth. Throbs like a fruit, over-ripe—spilling its milky juice into her mouth.

She dips the pen back into the inkbottle, withdraws its black tip, and writes on her inner thighs:

When your clitoris is the—of the match and my fingers are the matches. Words are like fingers that march fiercely into the labia of the paper, spreading

open the arena of ecstasy.

The conference room has a different tone. A hue my sight does not know how to comprehend. The teapot hisses. Steam floats out as I lift the lid. Grabbing the handle, time pours out and fills the brim of the ceramic mug. Jasmine floats in and out of my nose.

I walk toward the cabinet's drawer and pull out a garlic bulb. And begin to peel it.

In the conference room, a door opens. And closes. Like white culottes opening the curtain of their skirt. I think of the airport Charles de Gaulle. The window. The door. The bright afternoon light. Where flight attendants in miniskirts wheel their luggage to and fro. Where paintings are suspended from the ceiling. The Tree of Solitude. The House of Intimacy. The Vanishing Point of Color. Inside the conference room, you are wearing a blue blouse sitting perpendicular to me. Any closer and our shoulder blades would collide.

I cease telling you. Why I write. Why I read. I begin narrating to you the language of drawing and painting. With a piece of lithography. A piece of Japanese handmade paper the color of amber silver. I show you a piece of a horse. A woman. A head of a horse and a body of a woman. His mane is spread across a section of the landscape of the paper.

I look at you. And you hold the art piece with your fingers spreading out behind, and your thumb pinning the front. This is the thin pipe of ink. Where the music of passion and pain are blown out. She does not live in the wind family. String. Please.

Take me in.

Could you see where the artist places her hands on the ink stain? To produce different notes. Different ink glissandi. Watch as it spills out, cannot be contained by the instrument that creates it. Please.

Leave me here.

I watch you from my peripheral vision. As you listen to the composition. I wonder if you could see that there is the symmetry of desire manifesting.

From two lines merging, dividing out, mirroring each other in almost exact diffusion. There are other ink lines. Pipes that become systolic, desperate, intense, overwhelmed. In an attempt to create a woman. Sleeping. Dreaming. Reclining. In the midst of her orgasmic rage. Her head is transformed into a horse.

Oh! And trees!

And I contemplate if you notice. The two red solid masses of red. One square. One rectangular. Passion. Pain. Both diastolic. Filling the chambers red. Into basic geometric shapes. The red square. The red rectangular. Please. The red square is beneath the layer of ink, of her mane, of the writing that looks like musical notes on the top page. On the bottom of the page. Or the red rectangular that lies beneath her legs. Where her non-existent feet should be. Chaining her to her bed made out of. Pulp of wood. Pulp of cotton. Pulp of alfalfa, as she screams perhaps—

out of ecstasy out of despair out of confusion

And I look at you, looking for clues of your vision. You look at her as she is spread out. Of the handmade paper the color of amber silver. Her body the color of that too. Since she is nude. She has no value. She has no shadow. She is made out of strokes, ink pipes, out of a passionate rage. She is created. Made to syncopate with the fibrous strings. Of the paper. Fibrous strings that writhe out to every edge. Without a beginning. Without an ending. Like an ecstasy. Like a desire.

You whisper something I cannot recall or remember. And I think Renaissance.

I think of Boccaccio, Petrarch, Raphael. I think of madrigals. Polyphonic masses of Palestrina. Viols floating down the river of Florence.

language
opens

I think my pen can understand its language. The tongue that speaks the river of Renaissance.

And I wonder from that image of Florence if you could see the airport Charles

de Gaulle. You let the woman dressed in ink float down onto the surface of the table. You let the woman breathe a little. Be deranged a little. Be lightheaded a little.

You think of the world of Renaissance. You think you cannot contain her. You think this is the beginning of passion. You think it's a difficult language. I look at your blue blouse. Your long fingers. Your long hands.

Shall I tell you the history of why I draw. Why I paint. The canvas of my passion.

Shall I revive the experience for you?

How do you want it to be delivered? In lipsticks? In high heels?

I drew. I painted this piece because—

The woman I was seeing then. The woman with dark hair, black eyes, sweet lips Shaved her dark pubic hair Day and night

Un-decorating the region below. She shaved when she woke up in the morning, before having breakfast, always before having breakfast. She trimmed the bushes in mid-afternoon. After her long nap. She mowed the lawn before climbing into bed. She was a poet who enjoyed carving things and words.

She informed me, I need to get rid of this black forest. I am losing my way through.

When she had difficult with not being able to trim— when I told her to stop.

I let the ink drop sporadically on the page. To give voice to the hair as it scattered across the bathroom floor. With the pen tip, I mark strokes. Shaped the short scratches. Into confusion. Into ecstasy. Into despair. And she became a woman. I wrote on the paper: This is my consciousness. This is my consciousness. In writing.

But in the conference room, I do not tell you this story. This reason why. I say, I enjoy how drawing is an extension of

lines, and how lines become an instrument of writing. (Of desire—this I leave out)

This marriage is mine. Do you want to enter? This connubial gathering of hair?

You listen. And I listen to you listening.

And my heart halts in its glissando. I remember. I recall. The birth of creation. The ink was contracting. Systolic. Relaxing. Diastolic. You can see on the paper. It was once wet before dried, parched. A black glossy coating describing the ink time spent with ecstasy.

Sometimes I write too much. I need to write as little as possible.

Leaning my back against the Tree of Solitude. Two minutes of the forty-five minutes. It's eternity in the slit of time. Rilke's Solitude and Marriage. You are sitting close. The space that houses intimacy. Your back to the tree, mine to it too. Our hair—your blonde, my black—coils the pipes of the tree.

You are the sky and I am the lake. We take turns looking into each other's reflection.

Is this love? Aniseed—

The apples on the apple tree fall to the ground.

Let me take you into the fiber, the edge of my painting. Into the labia of the Stonehenge, the Kochi. Into the woody entrance of the paper skin.

Let me take you to the House of Intimacy. It lies across the bridge of the abyss. Hold my hand as I lead you across the quiet chasm. On Alphabet Land. Our naked feet spelling each word onto the palimpsest of desire.

In the House of Intimacy we do not experience will in any manner.

I am peeling, derobing the thin diaphanous skin of the garlic bulb. Shanghai in the background conversing with flowers. Oh Hsiao-hsien! Oh Hsiao-hsien! Opium comes and goes like Theodore Stevenson.

Let me peel the imminent face of death. Strip him bare. Strip him naked. A flake. A fragment. A sliver.

In time.

The white face of flake descends the carpet on the kitchen's floor. I am sipping

hot jasmine tea. You are tea. I must drink you. I must.
Spill you on my large Kochi canvas.

Each descending flake is a window into your world,
floating, dancing slowly downward. In phrasing a
moment. In undressing the past. I am thinking of the
fragment. The sliver. The door. The window. Looking
through.

You approached me once while driving. I was walking
to work. You noticed me crossing the light on
Alphabet Land. You pulled into someone's large
parking lot. You had just come from the fitness center.
I imagined you must have been up since 6:30. And I
thought you were one to indulge in sleep.

Do you want a ride to work? you asked, with no muffin-top hairdo, your hair down, and no makeup. It was a sight I remembered having enjoyed thoroughly. I regretted immediately assigning an automatic no thanks to your offering. At that time I valued solitude more than intimacy. I had not understood the language of balance.

In that moment you were not the boss in the professional uniform. You were you, and per-

haps more you than you.

Let me walk you out of this Tree of Solitude. Let me take you into the fiber, the edge of painting. Into the labia of the Stonehenge, the Kochi. Into the woody entrance of the paper skin.

Let me take you to the House of Intimacy. It lies across the bridge of the abyss. Darkness. Voluminous. Sexy.

Women with their pale breasts exposed fall as we depart the Tree of Solitude. They fall slowly and calmly. They float in the cold air. Suspended. Kissing the ground on their way down with the hems of their skirts. The crushing sound of their weight. Lubricating dry the outer rim of the earth's dank lips.

Have you ever gazed at Autumn and desired her?
Have you?

We turn back to look at the painting. The leaves of
Words spread open their polychromatic wings.
Women are raining from the sky, the Tree of Solitude.
The memory of the afternoon spent under the canopy
of Words with you. The pipes of passion branching,
singing deeply into the ears of our senses. Ink

droplets in strands become women. Women with their
bosoms exposed be-

come strands of ink droplets. Raining.

I ask you, Did you enjoy tasting Solitude with me? As we walk into the nebulous bosom of fog. Charles de Gaulle is very far away. The window. The door. The corridor. The silent sound of flight attendants in uniforms. The sky has darkened. Everything is dark blue.

The steam fills my entire body. The infusion of tea. My mind has become lucent and vast. Time, the Gentleman, has entered my soul through the crushed leaves of jasmine. He is holding his breath outside the palimpsest of desire. My breath expanding. I am looking out the window. I watch the shadows on the wall created by the blind, the diaphanous curtain, the window. A line-paged notebook is magnified on the wall, the light projector being the sun. I hanker to walk to the wall and write you a letter on it. I write with my black eyes, there is no bottom to this inkwell.

First Line: Who are you?

Second Line: Do you want to explore me, study me like a box, take me apart, and then re-

Third Line: assemble me? This sterile study, does it have intimacy in it? Is there spirituality too?

The Blue Fruit. Listening on the plate. Looking very luscious. The ambient noise of Shanghai muted by the intensity of my meditation. The television flickers like it has eyes.

The white skin of garlic descending. Raining. Falling. The window of the white world.

You are the sky and I am the lake. We take turns looking into each other's reflection.

Is this love? Aniseed—

In the conference room, a door opens. And closes. Like a white skirt opening the curtain of its culottes. Inside the conference room, you are wearing a blue blouse sitting perpendicular to me. Any closer and our shoulders collide.

I take you inside. You hold the drawing in the hand like a sheet of thin glass. As if the drawing is not empty and spindly. You read it quietly and slowly. From my peripheral gaze, it seems as if you could see through the artwork. As if it's transparent. It's a beauty to watch you read. The silent contour of art. Your long fingers like vines ex- tending forever. My head bent a little listening to you carefully. I must pay attention to symmetry, to the silent observation that escapes your reticent lips.

I think if Rodin were still alive, I would commission him to cast a piece of bronze and name it: *The Reader.* It would be you. I was in France once and visited the Musee Rodin on Varenne. It was remote and sadly, not a popular tourist site. An American man hovering near the entrance insisted that he purchase my entrance fee. He insisted that I bestow him the pleasure of paying for the Styx fee into the Gates of Hell. I did not have the heart to deny him. That pleasure. And when I entered Hell, it was something indeed. An aphrodisiac. Something Dante couldn't have related. Something provocatively erotic.

Like sadomasochism of heaven.

I did not know if it was the light angle from the camera, but *The Thinker* looked blue from the photo I printed out in Granada. The blue thinker did not alienate his thoughts from me as I suspected from the pamphlet I brought home from the museum. I remembered standing next to his blue body in the garden of the Hotel Biron, thinking he was not as beautiful as the Michelangelo's *David* I had seen in Florence. But his posture said everything that was on his mind. And I remembered desiring to climb on top of him, allowing him to insert his nonexistent blue phallus into me. To give him the permission to fire bullets of his solitude into my orifice. To watch as the seed of his thoughts spread out into my feminine consciousness. You would be the Reader, and you would come across very blue. I would climb on you differently, or perhaps not climb at all.

You continue to sit with that reading posture. A minute passes I believe. I divert my attention else where for fear of being caught with my pants on the ground. I begin to think: how does a woman desire another woman? Is it like with a man, the hankering to climb? A mountain, a tree, the skyscraper? Or something else less ascending, less gripping, less animalistic.

Perhaps, descend. Like falling. The way of women with exposed pale bosoms. I imagine descending you. Like an apple from an apple tree.

I had seen you the other day pulling into the corporation's driveway. The bus dropped me off at the light. I trudged up the broken pavement using the orange line as my walking ruler. A white semi whipped by lifting a blanket of red dust into the air. I grabbed my bag and dug my face into it

coughing. The foggy dust lingered mid-air before collapsing to the ground. There were clusters of dusty clouds suspended, not wanting to return to earth. I walked through it, my shoes digging into the small pebbles. There was a huge business sign up top saying Bob's Your Uncle. I always liked to think of the restaurant as Your Uncle is Bob. To my left a gas station, a T- shaped awning for raining days waiting for the bus to collect me.

Walking down hill and without any premonition. You saw me, smiled and waved. And I waved back. Wondered then looking at you. Looking at your car. I wondered if you have ever looked at a woman and desired her. What would that desire look like? It was a thought that crossed my mind for the first time. It was a beautiful one, I think.

More so. You are the superior in your professional uniform. You are.

I saw your silver car turning, becoming smaller and

then disappearing beneath the asphalt floor. The bright sun danced on its bituminous surface giving an illusion of a pool of water spilling into the dip in the road. I thought you and your car had submerged into a lake. For a brief moment, my heart jolted. Clearly you hadn't come to work

to commit suicide. The white flake, the white skin of garlic descends the stairs of air. Landing very

softly on the carpet. Defoliating like winter. I am walking with you across the bridge of the abyss. The passage between Solitude and Intimacy is a dark one. This quiet chasm of Death. Our naked feet spelling each word into the palimpsest of desire.

I am peeling off the imminent face of death. Strip him bare. Strip him naked. The seed of death. How it lives, thrives, relives in my mind. In my vision. What do you want me to do with this flower of death that has taken the shape of a garlic head? Blooming on the palm of my hands.

I would like to present you a flower growing from the garden of my mind. Will you take it? What will you do with it?

As I take you across the bridge of the abyss. My hand holding, leading yours. The House of Intimacy is on the other side. Flowers blooming from my mind onto yours.

Shanghai. The Blue Fruit hanging on the thin thread. Come here, You.

I talked to you once before flying over to Florida and Paris. I had not seen you in nine months. Where did you go? Are you coming? Continue to come? Inside my House of Intimacy? You informed me that I would love the Dali Museum in St. Petersburg. Where you were once its curator.

Email me, and I will give you directions. You said. Wearing black boots, black checkerboard pantyhose, black knee-high skirt. The color of your top, I did not remember. I believed there was a cathedral inside your blouse. You looked stunning. Should I feed you

Grapes Pears Anchovies? I felt religious. Votives. Cathedral.

I did not email you. But your Florida is gorgeous. The ocean. Its imperial vastness, its enigmatic potency, its irretrievable softness. This was once your home? Why did you not stay? You must leave too? You were faithful. To your husband, to your new job, to you, for the vicissitude you must make. For the ocean, I would be unfaithful.

They say that the universe is still expanding. That

the universe doesn't have an edge (being that the universe couldn't fall off itself, so to speak), yet it's limited. It's still forming itself. You must be the universe's antipode.

Tell me, how do I contain you? As I walk you across the bridge of the abyss. The conference room growing lighter. The teapot sitting very still on the burner. The red and blue tongue stop flickering. I am undressing the conversation in the kitchen

as Shanghai walks to and fro.

Beautiful panels. Brothel walls. Men consuming alcohol. And opium. And the dolor of Emerald and Pearl.

I say, Absorb me through your body of light. Let me taste your salty dissolving lips, milky forms that are in various states of becoming formlessness. You are forever folding into the edge of yourself, unfolding to release that bond into the edge of edgelessness.

Hallucinate with me, dream with me, become a part of me. You whisper.

We are walking in the dark between two cliffs. Our naked feet pressing on the synthetic resin of

the rope, tattooing diamond shapes and squares on their soft skin. Let me take you to the House of Intimacy.

Tree of Sounde

Contained emos

This is where God hangs the souls of the dead. On clotheslines stretching between one cliff and another cliff. One flimsy shirt of being against another being. Floating on wooden hangers. The shirts, white and bright, throw light on our path. We notice slippery shadows on our toes. The moonlight sifts through the branches dividing light off the leaves on the ground. The shadows of various incongruous things overlap each other, and the torment or equanimity they must feel having to exist in the same space with one another. There is hardly anyone out.

Over there the mountain. And below is the abyss.

Does He visit them, run his fingers across them like I would with my books, to see if they are still there? This is heaven. This is how God files the souls of the dead. On an outdoor closet.

Let us rest, I tell you. The journey is long.

We bend down and sit on the rope. You and I. Our legs dangling off the edge of the abyss.

We watch as the full moon gazes down at death,

the street without a name. She dips her face into the black water of the abyss. She takes a long exhalation before inhaling the spirits of the dead out of the darkness. We watch as she, the pallbearer, rides them through the clouds. A trail of steamed vapor floats beside her like a white silk scarf draped around her neck. She is misty and elegant. Being the phantom playing the night piano not with her fingers, but her lungs. Creating music of a translucent quality.

The shirt of the spirit flutters, an illusion of him breathing, inhaling with his lungs. But she is breathing for him, giving her last attempt of life to him. She throws him on the clotheslines. He hangs. With other souls. She is the spirit gravedigger.

This is God's vocation for her. We think.

Do you see your father out there on the clothesline? I ask. Your blue eyes searching. I will sit here with you and help you fish for your father's spirit. What shirt does he often wear?

I have never met him before. How white is his white shirt?

We sit quietly together. Our legs dangling off the edge of the abyss. I hear you breathing. I gaze at you softly. You stare out of the screen of nothingness. Your high chin faces the darkness, that hidden wall between our sobbing shoulders. You have a look as if you were about to walk into a Vermeer painting. To become a part of Dutch seventeenth-century antiquity. Perhaps you are. I am now sitting in front of this nocturnal canvas reading you like a painting. I can love you, I think. You sit there in that seahorse posture with me for hours, it seems. I do not know what stream of consciousness has taken you into its arms. But in that moment, I want to be a part of that riverbed. You can flow into me—and I can hold you. That stream of consciousness that is wider than me, longer than I can ever be. But I can hold you still. If you let me.

The silence of the evening is intoxicating. We sit there watching the moon. We stop taking counts of how many rounds she has made. One white shirt sandwiched between another white shirt. Immortal companions. What an ideal place for star-crossed lovers.

In the mist of fishing, Pyramus and Thisbe hanging on wooden hangers begin to converse with us. Their whiteness fluttering. No longer will they express their desire, passion, and affection through a wall. One thin fabric of their soul against another thin translucent fabric. Naked.

Mulberry Tree, Mulberry Tree, where art thou on this fall evening? Come, thy lips will no longer bear red or purple fruits.

What color dost thou want them to be?

It begins to rain. Small windows of pellets slicing through our skin. The lips of the dark sky must speak their mind. Even in the darkest hours. You think the moon has not gotten around to your father yet. I think we need more time. We think we must move forward or we will die of the cold. The rope of the bridge shakes as we quickly stand up. It's the bridge trembling or is it us?

I hold out my hand, your numbed cold hand locking mine. You feel like soaked paper. Rain brings attention to the climate of our bodies. We have been very chilly so very long. It suddenly hits us. The cold penetrating. Our fingers, toes, nipples are haunted. The raw air of the evening cuts through our skin like a dream through the spirit. We cannot feel our toes. They are a glob of clay alienating their existence from our minds.

You and I dash quickly down the bridge. The synthetic resin of rope quivering upon the landing of our naked feet. The abyss below frightens

us. Darkness hovers over us like a king. The white soul on the clothesline. The moon. Our North Star. I have spent an evening on the edge of the abyss with you.

Fishing.

The small, cold hand of rain pulverizes our bodies, digging, crushing its icy body into us. Soaking everything in its path. The abyss below frightens us.

Fear begins to gain access into the hardened bastion

of our psyche. Where is the steam of Jasmine Tea? I wonder.

The Red. Blue tongue. To walk through the cold, I think of trees in this dark alluring moment. Trees are my holy kimonos.

I imagine you that holy kimono. Rain soaking my white dress. Your blue blouse.

Tree, you must sing through your pipes. Or we will die in the cold.

I imagine you the tree facing fear. You are no longer a young sapling. You are older and wiser. You stand tall wearing your daedal kimono, as the design of the gown spreads out and up like branches.

I imagine you that tree facing fear. You are the roots lying supine and supple on the dank window of the earth. The soil. Rich earthly dark frightens you. You gaze down at her voluptuous darkness. You begin to imagine what could be lurking underneath. You fear dying. You fear suffocation. You fear drinking in its darkness. You think you cannot breathe. You think no life can live with this large darkness. But you turn over like a tree, your face sinking into the ground. You extend your million little fingers and dig deep into the soil. There is no light. And you are on your own.

You are the tree standing tall. You are your own beacon of light. You travel in this darkness for days.

Traveling miles and miles into the earth's soil. You will not flake into salt. You are not Lot's wife. You never think once to look or turn back. You are deep into the darkness of your fear. You are drinking in the fear. And you discover that you live. That you breathe more free because of it. You begin to live. You learn that fear is your mother. The milk you drink to extract nutrition for growth. You travel all corners of darkness conveying water and food to other plants. You are the photo synthesis of leaves and plants. You become the bearer of the beacon. You are the

beacon. Embracing fear you become this. This is you. The tree.

Standing tall. With depth. With character. With beauty. I think this is quite a sight.

I see you embracing darkness. With a will, wild solitude of your own. My heart tugs and pulls like a ribbon on a box. I see you embracing darkness and I hanker to wrap my soul around you.

You are the canopy. The awning that shelters me as we plunge through this darkness.

Rain clumsily clings to the fabric of our soaked clothes. An evening dying, drowning in the rain. The abyss does not frighten us. The House of Intimacy becomes the lighthouse in the sea of darkness. The brightest lighthouse of all lighthouses.

We enter it, drenched. In the House of Intimacy we do not experience will in any manner.

In the kitchen, I am undressing the interview. Light dances on the floor of my mind.

In the conference room, a door opens. And closes. Like white culottes opening the curtain of their skirt. I think of the airport Charles de Gaulle. The window. The door. The bright afternoon light. Where flight attendants in miniskirts wheel their luggage to and fro. Where paintings are suspended from the ceiling. The Tree of Solitude. The House of Intimacy. The Vanishing Point of Desire. Inside the conference room, you are wearing a blue blouse sitting perpendicular to me. Any closer and our shoulders collide.

Do you flinch or is it the fabrication of my mind? You flinch as the drawings float down the table. I do not think you flinch because you are cold. In the conference room. You flinch because, like me, you have starved yourself of touch. Of human contact. That you are sensitive to space, to intimacy. That you are a passionate women. And that perhaps an ounce of this contact, the contact between the paper and its pen, can make you delirious.

That your body wants something that your mind won't give. Give up so easy. That perhaps you want to have control of your desires.

That you dispense very little of it to yourself. We begin lighting candles and votives. I am inside the Cathedral. The House of Intimacy is a continuous space made of light. It's held up by four pillars of love. Pillar of Opening. Pillar of Desire. Pillar of Trust. Pillar of Vulnerability. In here, everything throbs. In here, the virtue of ecstasy robs reality of its synthetic robes.

Inside. Reality is naked. We face the white canopy bed. The diaphanous cloth drapes over its throne, flutters lightly like the heart of a woman. Reality is not limited to the motions of light. It is also a desire. This bedroom is my Library of Alexandria. Where we descend into knowledge, the fruit of passion, our carnal desire.

Let us undress the body of ecstasy.

You are the sky and I am the lake. We take turn looking into each other's reflection. I gaze into your blue eyes. I search and look and look at their windows.

I look and look. Deeply. Longingly. And find in their reflection—

That I have beautiful eyes. That my lips are quite luscious. That my body is alive. That this is a beautiful corpse to die in.

My hands dizzied. My heart throbs. The world is big. Very big.

I walk into you. You are completely drenched. I am too. The room begins to warm up.

Let me unbutton the shirt of your soul. Let me revel in your nakedness. Walk my tongue down your navel. And kiss the inner thighs that open your world to me.

Let me unbutton the shirt of your soul. Unfastening every inch of you. Come here. Let us. Shall we.

You and I against the oblique room. This fluttering canopy bed. This Library of Alexandria.

Inside the House of Intimacy, Time, the Gentleman, doesn't get to inspect or taste you. He stands outside the door, outside the palimpsest of desire, growing green and angry and wicked.

For two minutes I escort you through The Tree of Solitude. The House of Intimacy. The window into art. Into language. Into desire.

I remove one handbound book of much antiquity down from its shelf and lay it on the white canopy bed.

Rainwater drips down your blue blouse, my dress, your skirt. A pool on the ceramic floor reflects our dark passion.

A feat, I believe, impossible begins to unfold. I look into your eyes: the well of desire. Flowers bloom out of Shanghai.

Women with their bosoms exposed fall out of the sky. Trees are mesmerized. You open the window. The door. The corridor.

Two women stand facing one another inside a house. One shy and the other obliged. Gazing into each other's shyness.

Each gaze a window. A door. A corridor.

A vacuous raindrop on the ocean's floor. An empty silence. A button. Unbuttoned.

A silent drop.

I begin to unfasten your blue blouse. One button. One drop at a time.

Let me chisel the edge of passion with my tongue. I watch you as each button unfastens, and falls on the empty hands of dark- ness.

Each drop is an empty sound. A silent glissando. Each button. Each drop. Empty. Not emptiness. Into the well of longing.

Let me take you into the fiber. Into the edge of Intimacy. Into the labia of Kochi. Into the woody entrance of the paper skin. As I disrobe every inch of you. Every centimeter. Your black skirt coils down as it spills onto the ceramic floor. Like stairs.

The palimpsest of Desire opens up its ancient book. Your wet, black pantyhose peeling. Peeling. And peeling.

Your skirt, your pantyhose coiling out of you.

Inside the House of Intimacy we *do not* experience will in any manner. Inside the House of Intimacy we *must* experience will in *every* manner.

You draw me into your arms like water out of a well. Your hands dancing on my spine. Your hip pinning me to the canopy post. Your hip, a kiss on my gender, pinning me. Delicious kiss. Your legs, ropes, cords, fibers begin to knot my body.

You look into my eyes before tearing me apart, tightening the ropes of our desires.

Are you knitting? A slit. A rip. A knot.

You begin to remove the dress off my cold body. I tremble upon your touch. You lift it slowly over my head. The hem curling upward like the slender stems of—vines, clouds.

You draw me into your arms like water out of a well. Your long fingers burn on my skin. Your hip pinning me to the canopy post. Your hip, a kiss on my gender, pinning me. Delicious kiss. Your legs, fingers, ropes, cords, fibers begin to knot my body.

You are the sky, I am the lake. We take turns gazing into each other's reflections. A drop of desire ripples out of the center of sky. Water, waves flutter out of the center of the lake.

Water. Nipples. Lake. It's snowing. Snowing. And snowing.

We begin gripping each other's body. The drapes
fluttering. The votives burning. The candles flickering.
Its blue, red tongue into the labia of darkness. I pin
you to the bed. Crushing you with the small hands of
tenderness. My tongue digging into your skin. My
tongue is a river spilling its entire contents on the
ocean of your body.

The fiber of paper skin ripping ripping ripping.

My tongue grips your thighs like a pen, like a rope.
Writing and roping you—

as you scream in ecstasy. Each strand, each fiber of you ripped into pieces. Threads. Strings. Motif.

You are experiencing the language of Authenticity. Inside the House of Intimacy we experience will in *every* manner.

I spread open the labia of the palimpsest with 66 my tongue. My fingers. My pen nib.

The antique book is a journal. Made out of fine, rare paper. A journal of want and desire. A woman lies on the canopy bed—

No— You lie on the canopy bed with fluttering white drapes. No—

A handmade journal lies on my bed like a woman. Like a desire. Like a door. An elongated strip of yellow lace, your/her hair perhaps, loops around your/her body several times through a small punctured orifice the size of a small ink drop. Attached to your/her back, a small rectangular flap peeks out as a penholder. Two white tissue bookmarks tuck inside your/her body like a tenon wedged through a mortise. You are/she is bathed in the room of light. Is languishing on my bed.

I want to bang on her/your door— with the knob of my pelvis, the knobs of my breasts 67 Let me in. Inside you/her. I want to—

make love to you/her with the tip of my pen. Dip you and her in ink. Write on your body on her. Over and over with my thoughts. My dreams. My passion. The pen's tongue moves like a lizard. Like a river

on the milky body. Edging on each shore with black tears, black pain, black

desire.

I move toward her into you and hold you on her on the palm of my hand. I begin to unfasten her/your black bra. Unlace her until she is naked, and free, and opened.

I open her/you like a door quietly but with great urgency

You are/she is spread open wider than the sea, wider than the horizon, wider—

to receive the river of my pen. Let me dip you in ink one inch at a time. Let me dip you. Dip you. Dip you. Oh you sensuous lover of sensuous proportions. Oh, let me dip you.

Your opal dancing upon my touch. Dancing. Singing. Inside of darkness.

Inside the House of Intimacy. Barren and naked. You draw me into your arms. Your eyes deeply into mine. We are as dark as sorrow. As bright as light.

Let me undress the shirt of your soul. Let me revel in your nakedness. Walk my tongue down your navel. And kiss the inner thighs that open your world to me.

Let me unbutton the shirt of your soul. Unfastening every inch of you.

Each button. A silent drop into the well of desire. Each button. Each kiss of heaven.

Your eyes gazing into mine. With one gaze, you slit my soul open. Your piercing blue eyes dancing. Must you pierce me like that, I ask you? Must you?

My tongue, a pen, its nib digging digging digging

into your soul, stroking a black mark on your skin. A memory of its time spent with ecstasy. I am the riverbed. You are the river, the consciousness, that flows into my arms.

We are one. A button. A silent drop.

I lay the naked garlic on the table, completely defoliated of its winter. White skin. And begin to wrap my fingers around the Blue Fruit. There are flakes of snow on the carpet. Flowers are blooming out of brothel panels. Shanghai is walking to and fro like Theodore Stevenson. Opium drifting. Shifting its point of ecstasy.

I take my first bite into you. I feel diabolically hypnotic. I dash around the house in slow motion, a silent film, opening all the windows and pulling up the blind halfway. Light becomes a child quivering, dissolving upon my touch. Darkness is about to arrive. I crack open the lid of night. I take a bite into you. The smell of fresh mowed grass, an alluring scent of parsley and aniseed. I hear the wheels on the asphalt. Silhouettes of solitude flutter out with the artificial light emitting from the ceiling's chandelier. In exchange, darkness enters, with her gown of sensuality and timelessness. She floats inside and sits down like a guest.

I take my first bite into you. Eating you. My eyes searching the horizon for the Vanishing Point of Desire. Nowhere in sight. Desire doesn't have a point. It doesn't vanish.

book
about
nowhere
enjoy
love

This is my third painting. My complete exhibition. Will you let me know what you think of it? As you descend out of the airport Charles de Gaulle. As you walk out of the conference room from the interview.

Flowers of Shanghai. Do they ever bloom out of your television screen? And make you enter the Cathedral? Leave a mark on your skin?

VI KHI NAO was born in Long Khanh, Vietnam, in 1979. In 2013, she graduated with an MFA in fiction from Brown University, where she received the John Hawkes and Feldman Prizes in fiction and the Kim Ann Arkstark Memorial Awards in poetry. Vi's work includes poetry, fiction, film and cross-genre collaboration. She is the author of two novellas, *Swans In Half-Mourning* (2013) and *The Vanishing Point of Desire* (2011), and was the winner of 2015 Nightboat Poetry Prize.